Dear Mabel!

Written and Illustrated by
Pat Cummings

Celebration Press
An Imprint of Pearson Learning

Dear Mabel, dear Mabel,

there's pie on the table.

Can you come over for tea?

3

Dear Molly, dear Molly,

thank you for the note.

I'll wear my new scarf

if I come in my boat.

Dear Mabel, dear Mabel,

there's fruit on the table.

Can you come over for tea?

Dear Molly, dear Molly,

my new hat from Spain

is just right to wear

if I'm coming by train.

Dear Mabel, dear Mabel,

there's milk on the table.

Can you come over for tea?

11

Dear Molly, dear Molly,

let's hope it won't rain.

I'll wear my new dress

if I come in my plane.

Dear Mabel, dear Mabel,

the cat's on the table!

Are you coming over for tea?

15

Dear Molly, dear Molly,
thank you for the card.
I'll put on my shoes
and RUN to your yard!

16